THE HUNTER'S PROMISE

An Abenaki Tale

By

Joseph Bruchac

Illustrated by

Bill Farnsworth

✤Wisdom Tales✤

Wisdom Tales is an imprint of World Wisdom, Inc.

Library of Congress Cataloging-in-Publication Data

Bruchac, Joseph, 1942-
  The hunter's promise : an Abenaki tale / by Joseph Bruchac ;
illustrated by Bill Farnsworth.
    pages cm
  Audience: Grades K-3.
  ISBN 978-1-937786-43-4 (hardcover : alk. paper) 1. Abenaki
Indians--Folklore--Juvenile literature. I. Farnsworth, Bill,
illustrator. II. Title.
  E99.A13.B782 2015
  974.004'9734--dc23

                                                      2015009727

Printed in China on acid-free paper.

Production Date: April 2015,
Plant & Location: Printed by 1010 Printing International Ltd,
        Job/Batch #: TT15030518

For information address Wisdom Tales, P.O. Box 2682,
Bloomington, Indiana 47402-2682
www.wisdomtalespress.com

Author's Note

The Hunter's Promise is my own retelling of a traditional story that can be found in various forms among a great many of the indigenous nations of the Northeast, both Iroquoian and Algonquin.

A version entitled "Story of Team, the Moose," appears in the 1897 collection *In Indian Tents, Stories told by Penobscot, Passamaquoddy and Micmac Indians* by Abby L. Alger. A similar telling, entitled "The Moose Wife" was included in the *Thirty-Second Annual Report of the Bureau of American Ethnology, 1910-1911*, a large collection of tales gathered around 1888 by Jeremiah Curtin from esteemed elders of the Seneca Nation in western New York State.

In addition to such written sources, my telling owes a debt to a number of tradition bearers who were my elders, including the late Msawelasis (Maurice Dennis) and Atian Lolo (Stephen Laurent), as well as contemporary Wabanaki tellers such as our friend Roger Paul.

The story may be seen as a tale about loyalty and trust—keeping a promise to one's family. It is certainly that. However, on another level, it is also about the proper relationship of humans to the natural world.

It's long been understood among the Wabanaki,* the people of the dawn land, that a bond exists between the hunter and those animals whose lives he must take for his people to survive. It is more than just the relationship between predator and prey. When the animal people give themselves to us, we must take only what we need and return thanks to their spirits. Otherwise, the balance will be broken. Everything suffers when human beings fail to show respect for the great family of life.

Joseph Bruchac

* The nations included in the Wabanaki Confederacy are the Abenaki, Maliseet, Mi'kmaq, Passamaquoddy, and Penobscot.

Long ago in the forests of the northeast, there was a young man who was a fine hunter. Each fall he would go deep into the forest to the north. There he would make his camp and stay throughout the winter, hunting. Then in the spring he would return to his village with his canoe full of dried meat and animal skins.

But, one winter as he was following the tracks of a moose, he realized something. He was lonely. "I wish I had a partner," he said.

That night, when he came back to his lodge, he was surprised at what he found. The fire was burning. The lodge had been cleaned. Food had been cooked and served into a wooden bowl for him. Yet he saw no one in the lodge. After eating that food, he was very tired and fell asleep. When he awoke next morning, more food had been prepared for him. However, there was still no one to be seen.

So it went, day after day. He would wake up each morning and find food waiting for him. Then he would go hunting. When he returned at night he would find everything in order and more food waiting. The animal skins from the day before would be scraped and prepared for tanning. The meat would be hung on drying racks.

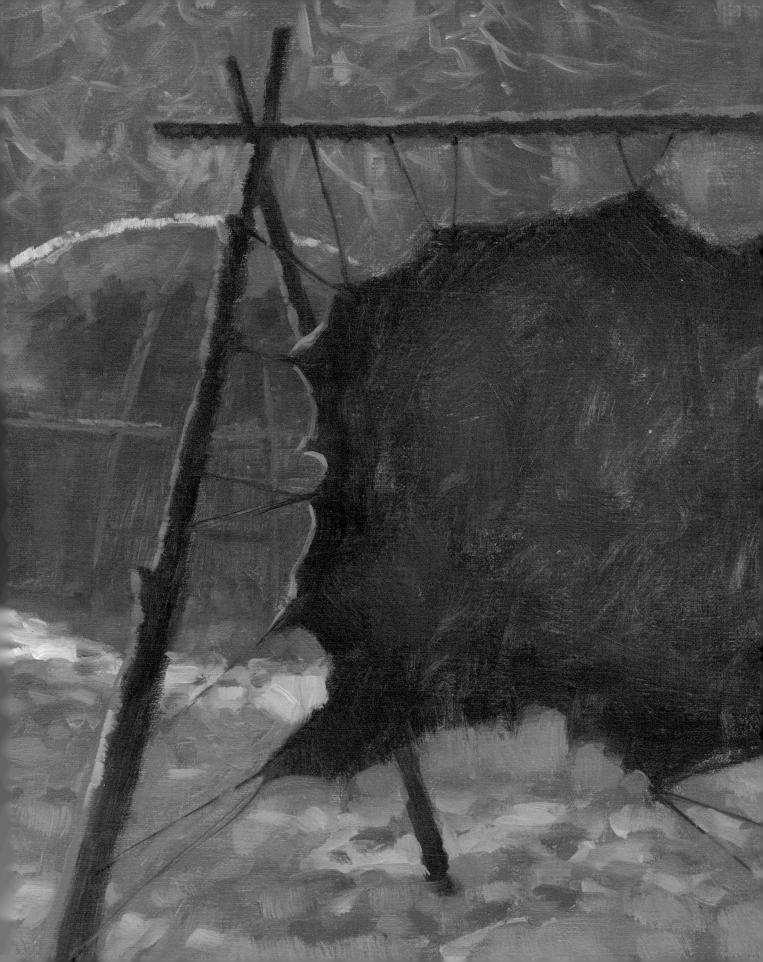

Finally, on the seventh night, he found a woman waiting in the lodge when he returned. She did not speak, but she served his food to him. Then she made her bed next to his, still without saying a word. Respecting her silence, he also never said a word.

So it went all winter. Finally spring came. As he packed the canoe for the journey back to his village, she spoke.

"*Mikwalmi*," she said. "Promise to remember me."

"I promise," the hunter said.

Then she turned and walked back into the forest.

When that young man reached his village, his parents were happy to see him. They were pleased at how well he had done. He had brought back more meat and skins than ever before.

"My son," his father said, "I have found a fine young woman. She will make a good wife for you."

But the young hunter remembered the words spoken to him by the woman who had shared his lodge all that winter. He shook his head.

When fall came, he traveled again up the river to his winter camp. There he found his lodge waiting for him. And in front of his lodge stood that woman and a small boy.

"My husband," she said, "this is your little son. His name is Wadzo."

With a smile on his face, the young hunter stepped forward. He embraced his wife and their son.

It went just like the winter before. Each day, when he awoke, he found food prepared by his wife. Each night, when he came home, everything was in order. The skins had been scraped, the meat was drying, food was waiting for him.

One thing, however, was different. That son of theirs was not like other boys. Each morning, when the hunter awoke, he saw that Wadzo had grown. He had grown in one night as much as another child would grow in a year or more. By the seventh morning, Wadzo was no longer a little boy. He was a grown man. He was now strong enough to hunt with his father.

Together they did very well. When spring came, the hunter had twice as many skins and twice as much food to take back to the village.

"*Mikwalniona*," his wife said as she stood with their son by the river bank. "Promise to remember us."

"I promise," the hunter said.

Then the two of them turned and walked back into the forest.

This time when the hunter returned to the village everyone was impressed. The *sagamon*, the chief of the village, came up to him.

"I would like you to marry my daughter," he said.

But the hunter had not forgotten what his wife said to him. Just as before, he shook his head.

The chief's daughter, though, was a young woman who always got whatever she wanted. She had a powerful *poohegan*, a spirit helper. And as that young man was walking along the next morning, that *poohegan* in the shape of a Canada jay flew up. It fluttered its wings in front of his face. A cloud filled his mind and covered every memory of his wife and their son.

So he married the chief's daughter. He no longer smiled and often seemed distant and confused. However, his new wife was pleased. She had gotten what she wanted.

When fall came and it was time for him to go again to the north, the chief's daughter stood looking at the hunter and his canoe.

"My husband," she said, "You must take me with you."

Because he could not refuse, he nodded his head and she climbed in. Then he took up his paddle to begin the long journey.

At last they reached the place where he always camped. The hunter climbed from the canoe. He walked up the hill to his campsite, followed by the chief's daughter. There was his lodge. In front of it stood his winter wife and their grown son. With them was a young man.

"This is your second son," she said. "His name is Sibo."

As soon as he saw them, the cloud left the hunter's mind. He knew them to be his wife and his children.

"Ah," his winter wife said. "You did not keep your promise."

Then she and the two boys began to walk away. As they entered into the forest, they turned into three moose.

The hunter turned to the chief's daughter. "You tricked me!" he said.

Then he walked to the edge of the forest. There he drove his ax deep into the trunk of a spruce tree. He hung his snowshoes from that ax and disappeared into the snowy forest.

The chief's daughter tried to follow him. But the man's footprints in the snow soon vanished. All she could find were the tracks of *iawak mozak*—four moose.